Mule Eggs

A Richard Jackson Book

MULE EGGS

by Cynthia DeFelice

pictures by Mike Shenon

Orchard Books
New York

For all my nieces and nephews—
Hadley and Simon, Michelle and Tony,
Peter and Katie, Shelly and Thomas,
Will and Ava
                    —C.DeF.

For Harold M. Kramer, who
taught me how
                    —M.S.

Text copyright © 1994 by Cynthia DeFelice
Illustrations copyright © 1994 by Mike Shenon

Orchard Books
95 Madison Avenue
New York, NY 10016

Manufactured in the United States of America
Printed by Barton Press, Inc.
Bound by Horowitz/Rae
Book design by Mike Shenon

10 9 8 7 6 5 4 3 2 1

The text of this book is set in 19 point Bembo Bold.
The illustrations are mixed media, predominantly
ink line and oil pastel.

Library of Congress Cataloging-in-Publication Data
DeFelice, Cynthia C.
    Mule eggs / by Cynthia DeFelice ; pictures by Mike Shenon.
        p.   cm.
    "A Richard Jackson book"—Half t.p.
    Summary: Patrick the city slicker, a new farm owner, falls prey to
a practical joke but is able to turn the tables on his deceiver.
    ISBN 0-531-06843-9.—ISBN 0-531-08693-3 (lib. bdg.)
    [1. Farm life—Fiction.   2. Practical jokes—Fiction.]
I. Shenon, Mike, ill.   II. Title.
PZ7.D3597Mu   1994   [E]—dc20   93-49395

When Patrick moved from the city to the country and bought himself a farm, the other farmers shook their heads.

"He's a city slicker," they said, "and the city is where he belongs."

"He doesn't know a pitchfork from a plow," they said.

"He doesn't know which end of a cow to milk!" they said.

"He wouldn't know beans if his head was in the pot," they said.

They all agreed that Patrick would never make it as a farmer, but a farmer is what Patrick wanted to be.

Now Patrick had noticed that all the other farmers owned at least one mule. So one fall day Patrick headed to the market to buy one for himself.

By and by he passed a farmer who was working in his pumpkin patch.

"Good day to you, neighbor," called Patrick.

"Well, if it isn't Patrick," answered the farmer. "Are you on your way back to the city?"

"Oh no," said Patrick. "I'm off to the market to buy me a mule."

"A mule, you say?" asked the farmer.

"That's right," said Patrick, looking around at all the pumpkins ripening in the field. Patrick had never seen pumpkins growing before. "How'd you grow such big orange apples?" he asked the farmer. "And, come to think of it, where's the tree?"

The farmer grinned to himself. "Why, Patrick, those aren't apples."

"They're not?"

"No," said the farmer. "They're eggs."

"Oh, eggs!" said Patrick. "What kind of eggs?"

"Mule eggs."

"Mule eggs! You mean to tell me your mule laid those?" asked Patrick.

"Yes, indeed," said the farmer.

"You mean to tell me a little baby mule is going to hatch out of each of those eggs?"

"Yessiree."

The farmer reached down and picked up a big pumpkin. He felt it carefully. "This one's nice and ripe," he said. He held it up to his ear and listened. "Yep, I can hear the little feller in there kicking. You want to buy it?"

"Oh yes!" cried Patrick. "I surely would like a little baby mule colt. But how much does a mule egg cost?"

"Well," said the farmer, "this one here, now, I reckon I could let you have it for only twenty-five dollars—seein' as it's you, Patrick."

Patrick happily paid the farmer twenty-five dollars. Now I'll have my mule and money left over, too! he thought.

As Patrick carried his mule egg down the road, the farmer called after him, "Remember now, Patrick, an egg has to stay warm. Wrap some blankets around it to make a little nest. And you'll have to sit on it, of course, just like a mama mule. Watch it real careful—it's about ready to hatch!"

Patrick went hurrying home to put his mule egg in a nice warm place. But he was so excited that he didn't watch where he was going and he tripped over a log and stubbed his toe.

The pumpkin went flying out of his arms and
went rolling down the hill!
It rolled

      and it bounced

           and it landed

right in the middle of a big brier patch.

Ker-plat!

It smashed against a rock and busted wide open.

Patrick watched his egg break. Just then a rabbit, frightened by the crashing, rolling pumpkin, ran out of the other side of the brier patch.

"My baby mule!" hollered Patrick. He began chasing that rabbit from one brier patch to another calling, "Here, little muley! Here, little muley! Come back to Patrick. Come to your mama!"

But no matter how fast he ran, Patrick couldn't catch that rabbit. Finally he gave up.

He walked back down the road and said to the farmer, "Of all the bad luck! The egg hatched before I could get it home, and that little baby mule was so fast I couldn't catch it."

"Would you like to buy another?" asked the farmer greedily.

"Could I?" asked Patrick, reaching into his pocket for another twenty-five dollars. "Only this time, give me one that's not quite so ripe."

The farmer put the money in his pocket. "Here, take this," he said, handing Patrick another pumpkin. "I think there're twins in this one."

"Twins!" said Patrick. "Imagine that."

The farmer watched Patrick walk away with his egg. What a noodlehead, he thought.

Patrick built a nest in the barn and began sitting.

He sat . . .

and he sat . . .

and he sat . . .

but nothing happened.

He sat . . .

and he sat . . .

and he sat some more . . .

but still nothing happened.

As he sat, Patrick looked around the barnyard. He watched the chickens and ducks and barn swallows, all sitting on their nests. He watched the pigs and the cows and the horses. Not one of them was sitting on a nest.

Suddenly Patrick felt very foolish. He jumped off the nest crying, "People don't sit on nests... and *mules don't hatch from eggs!* That farmer is trying to make a goose out of me."

Patrick went into the house and thought for a long, long time. "Maybe I am a city slicker," he said to himself, "but I know a few tricks, too."

Patrick mixed together some water and grape juice in a small bottle, shook it well, and put it in his pocket. Then he got his last fifty dollars, went to the market, and bought himself two baby mule colts. On the way home, he made sure to pass by the farmer's field.

The farmer looked up and saw Patrick with his two beautiful baby mules. "Where did you get the mules, Patrick?" he called.

"From the egg you sold me—where else?" answered Patrick. "And you were right. There were twins in there! Aren't they fine looking?"

The farmer couldn't believe his eyes and ears. "Wait, Patrick!" he called. "You're not trying to tell me you got those mules out of that pump— I mean, that *egg* I sold you, are you?"

"Yes," replied Patrick, "of course. Isn't that what you said would happen?"

"Well, y-yes," said the farmer.

"But," Patrick continued, "it didn't work quite the way you said it would."

"It didn't?" the farmer asked, beginning to feel confused.

"No," said Patrick. "I sat on the egg like you told me to do, but nothing happened. I was just about to give up when I remembered my transmogrification potion."

"Say that again," said the farmer. "Your *what*?"

"My transmogrification potion," said Patrick, pulling the bottle out of his pocket. "I don't know why I didn't use it in the first place."

"What's transmog—whatchacallit potion?" asked the farmer.

"You mean you've never heard of it?" said Patrick with astonishment. "People in the city have been using it for years."

"But what does it do?" the farmer asked.

"It's very scientific," said Patrick. "You see, it works according to the principles of frivolity and obscurity. It can create an entirely new object simply by changing gleeps into bleeps."

The farmer looked bewildered.

"But you don't need to understand all that big city talk," said Patrick with a smile. "It's very simple to use. When I rubbed some of the potion on the egg you sold me, it transmogrified into my twin mules here."

Patrick looked around at all the pumpkins still lying in the field. "With a little bit of this stuff, you could have a whole herd of mules. You'd be rich!"

Patrick turned and began leading his mules home.

"Patrick!" called the farmer. "Wait. Have you, uh, got any of that—that stuff for sale?"

"Well . . . I suppose I could spare a bottle . . . ," said Patrick. "Seeing as it's you."

"How much?" asked the farmer, reaching quickly into his pocket.

"Fifty dollars a bottle," answered Patrick. "But that's nothing to a man who's about to become rich!"

The farmer handed Patrick fifty dollars. "I just rub it on the pumpkins, er, I mean the eggs, is that right?" he asked.

"Yes, but there's one more thing," said Patrick. "You must let the eggs know what you want them to transmogrify into. In this case, it's very easy. Every time you rub an egg with the potion, simply say, 'Hee-haw, hee-haw.' "

"Hee-haw, hee-haw?" asked the farmer. "Like that?"

"Yes, but you should try to sound a little more ornery. You know, stubborn, like a mule."

"Hee-haw! Hee-haw!" cried the farmer, frowning stubbornly. "Hee-haw!"

"That's better," replied Patrick, smiling. "It takes a while to work, so don't give up. Keep at it until you've got all the mules you want."

"Oh, I will," said the farmer. "I will!" He
began rubbing the potion on a large pumpkin
and braying, "Hee-haw! Hee-haw!"

The farmer's bellows followed Patrick and his baby mules as they walked on down the road toward home.

That night when Patrick climbed into bed, he could hear that the farmer was still hard at work: "Hee-haw! Hee-haw! Hee-haw!"

As for Patrick, he named his little mule colts Tit for Tat and That's That, and folks say he's doing right well as a farmer, after all.